Dear Parent:
Your child's love of reading starts here!

Every child learns to read in a different way and at his or her own speed. Some go back and forth between reading levels and read favorite books again and again. Others read through each level in order. You can help your young reader improve and become more confident by encouraging his or her own interests and abilities. From books your child reads with you to the first books he or she reads alone, there are I Can Read Books for every stage of reading:

SHARED READING
Basic language, word repetition, and whimsical illustrations, ideal for sharing with your emergent reader

BEGINNING READING
Short sentences, familiar words, and simple concepts for children eager to read on their own

READING WITH HELP
Engaging stories, longer sentences, and language play for developing readers

READING ALONE
Complex plots, challenging vocabulary, and high-interest topics for the independent reader

ADVANCED READING
Short paragraphs, chapters, and exciting themes for the perfect bridge to chapter books

I Can Read Books have introduced children to the joy of reading since 1957. Featuring award-winning authors and illustrators and a fabulous cast of beloved characters, I Can Read Books set the standard for beginning readers.

A lifetime of discovery begins with the magical words **"I Can Read!"**

*Visit www.icanread.com for information
on enriching your child's reading experience.*

I Can Read!

BEGINNING 1 READING

Pinkalicious™

Pink around the Rink

To Maeve, Gareth, Nancy, and Kevin
—V.K.

The author gratefully acknowledges
the artistic and editorial contributions
of Daniel Griffo and Susan Hill.

I Can Read Book® is a trademark of HarperCollins Publishers.

Pinkalicious: Pink around the Rink
Copyright © 2010 by Victoria Kann

PINKALICIOUS and all related logos and characters
are trademarks of Victoria Kann. Used with permission.

Based on the HarperCollins book *Pinkalicious* written by
Victoria Kann and Elizabeth Kann, illustrated by Victoria Kann
All rights reserved. Printed in the United States of America.
No part of this book may be used or reproduced in any manner whatsoever without
written permission except in the case of brief quotations embodied in critical articles and reviews.
For information address HarperCollins Children's Books, a division of HarperCollins Publishers,
10 East 53rd Street, New York, NY 10022.
www.icanread.com

Library of Congress catalog card number: 2010012633
ISBN 978-0-06-192880-2 (trade bdg.) —ISBN 978-0-06-192879-6 (pbk.)

11 12 13 LP/WOR 10 9 8 7 6

First Edition

I Can Read!

BEGINNING
1
READING

Pinkalicious™
Pink around the Rink

by Victoria Kann

HARPER
An Imprint of HarperCollinsPublishers

Yesterday,

Mommy gave me a big surprise.

It was a pair of brand-new

ice skates!

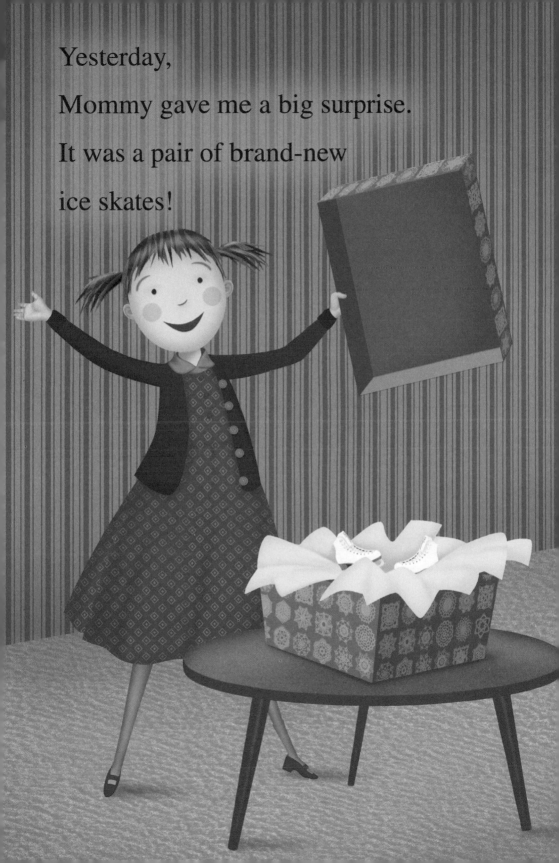

"Do you like them?" Mommy asked.

"I like them," I told her.

But there was one thing I did not like.

My new skates were not pink.

They were not purple,

or blue, or even green.

My new skates were boring old white.

"I can fix that," I said to myself.

I got my markers.

I picked out the color called

cotton candy pink,

and I colored my skates all over.

I was very careful.

Ta-da!

They looked pinkatastic.

Now I loved my new skates.
And I loved how I looked
in my new skates.

I couldn't wait

to go to the rink.

I would glide and spin.

I would be so graceful

in my cotton candy skates.

We went to the rink
the very next day.

"Your skates!" said Mommy.

"They're pink!" said Daddy.

"Cotton candy pink," I said.

I smiled.

17

Mommy did not
exactly smile.
Daddy smiled a little,
I think.

"Ready?" asked Daddy.

"Ready!" I said.

I was ready

to glide and spin!

I was not ready to wobble and fall.

But that is what I did.

I wobbled and fell again and again

and again.

Ouch!

But my sore bottom

wasn't the worst part.

The worst part was that
every time I fell,
my cotton candy skates
left cotton candy spots
and streaks all over the ice.
Everyone saw.

I started to cry a little.

Okay, a lot.

"Are you all right?" Mommy asked.

"I cry when something hurts, too,"
Daddy said.

"It's not that," I wailed.

"Look!" I pointed at my trail

of cotton candy pink

and my wet, messy skates.

Mommy smiled at me.

"The ice is pretty.

And your skates are one of a kind,

Pinkalicious," she said.

"Just like you."

I looked at my skates again.
Shades of pink dripped
and swirled and swooped
all over them.

Mommy was right.

My skates looked fantastic.

I was ready to try again.

Daddy skated with me
and held on to my hand.
This time I didn't
wobble and fall.
I was very graceful!

"That was fun!"
I said when
we got home.

"I'm glad," said Mommy,
"because I signed you up
for skating lessons!"

My new skates and I can hardly wait

to go skating again!